THE Party PRINCESS BOOK

Favourite Happy Ever After Stories
...and more!

By Janet Hoggarth

Illustrated by Caroline Glicksman

The Chicken House

To my darling Pete,
who will always be my Prince Charming – *JH*

To Bernard – *CG*

© 2002 The Chicken House

Illustrations © 2002 Caroline Glicksman
Text © 2002 Janet Hoggarth
Rollerblades is a registered trademark of Benetton Sportsystem USA, INC. (NJ Corp.).
The publishers would like to thank Olivia Luttrell for her help with Rapunzel's hair.

First published in the United Kingdom in 2002 by
The Chicken House, 2 Palmer Street, Frome, Somerset, BA11 1DS

Printed and bound in Singapore

British Library Cataloguing in Publication Data available.
Library of Congress Cataloguing in Publication Data available.

ISBN: 1 903434 54 8

Contents

Introduction

So, you want to be a princess? Let's see!

Are you *independent* like Rapunzel, or *free-thinking* like Sleeping Beauty? Are you *kind and considerate* like Beauty, or *sensitive* like Daisy (bruised by a pea)? Perhaps you're a *home-maker* like Snow White or have *inner beauty and small feet* like Cinderella.

Hmm . . . if you're not sure, read on.

Here are six favourite princess stories, all told with warmth and humour – a wonderful whirlwind of wishes and kisses, giggles and tiaras! And accompanying each story are some *special* princess party ideas – from hair tips by Rapunzel to Snow White's party bites!

But here's a secret! There's a princess in all of us, just waiting to be set free! And you don't need a fairy godmother with a magic wand to make your dreams come true – you can make them happen yourself.

Discover the princess in you, and sprinkle a little sparkle and happiness wherever you go!

1
Sleeping Beauty

"What about my christening gift to your precious baby?" cackled a voice at the back of the grand cathedral.

Everyone turned round to see who was speaking. A gasp rippled through the congregation. It was Esmerelda, the wickedest fairy of them all!

"You're not invited!" boomed Harold, the king.

"I am now! She's been given beauty, wit and talent by your *invited* fairy guests but I shall give the finest gift of all. On her sixteenth birthday, your darling daughter will prick her finger on a spinning wheel spindle and . . . DIE!" And she sent a bolt of lightning directly at the crib. The baby princess started crying immediately.

"No!" cried the queen, and crumpled in a dead faint on the floor. The king ran to her side and looked up at the toothless Esmerelda.

"I'll give you anything, you name it, it's yours! Please reverse the spell."

"I don't want anything – except your broken heart!" she spat.

A wild wind whirled up around her, making people hold on to their hats for fear they might blow away. But they didn't, because as soon as it had started, the wind stopped and she was gone. All that was left was the stench of rotten eggs.

Choking, the king spotted six fairies hovering around the crib of his baby daughter, Briar Rose, as if to protect her.

"All my fairy sisters have bestowed their gifts, but I still have mine to give," squeaked a voice from behind a purple velvet curtain at the head of the altar. The king and now the queen, who had just woken up, looked towards the altar to see who was speaking. Freya, the most practical fairy in the kingdom, fluttered up to the crib.

"My magic isn't as powerful as Esmerelda's, but I can at least change the spell. Shall I proceed?"

"Yes! Yes please, Freya. Do whatever you can," said the king.

Freya took out a handful of golden fairy dust from a little blue bag tied round her waist and kissed it.

"With this gift I protect Briar Rose from evil. Instead of dying on her sixteenth birthday, she shall fall into a deep sleep for a hundred years, and will only be woken by a kiss from her true love." And Freya sprinkled the dust over the baby's crib.

11

The king cleared his throat to make an announcement. "From this day on, it shall be against the law of this land to own a spinning wheel. Starting tomorrow, we will burn every last one till none remain. This way, the curse will never happen." So the next day there was a bonfire of spinning wheels as tall as the cathedral spire.

Over the next sixteen years, the princess grew up in the palace and enjoyed all the gifts bestowed upon her by the good fairies at her christening. She was a brilliant musician and a wonderful athlete. She had a mind as sharp as a razor and she could sing like an angel. She made the best chocolate cake in the universe and was as beautiful as a starlit night with the perfect number of freckles on her nose. But, despite all these gifts, the princess was bored!

Being cooped up day and night in a palace might be some people's idea of heaven, but not Briar Rose. Every time she asked: "But *why* can't I go to my best friends' parties?" the king would answer: "Rose, the law states that you can't leave the palace until *after* you are sixteen."

The week before her sixteenth birthday, Briar Rose sat down and made the invitations for a sleepover party. The king had promised she could celebrate in style, so she made invitations no one could resist – tiaras made of gold card with sparkling stuck-on rubies!

After days of elephants trampolining in her tummy and sleepless nights, the big day finally arrived. *The only present I want is the key to the palace gate, so I can ride a horse bareback through the woods, or swim across the palace moat,* she thought as she roller-bladed down to her birthday breakfast.

Lost in dreams of freedom, she whizzed down a passageway that normally took her out to the courtyard. As she braked, she noticed a small door in the wall that had never been there before. It was slightly ajar. *Hmm, I wonder where this leads*, she thought, intrigued. The princess had spent sixteen years exploring the palace and was sure she knew the place inside out. She pushed the little door open and, still wearing her roller blades, climbed up the stairs in front of her. At the top, Briar Rose found a tiny room where a gnarled old lady sat, spinning.

"Hello. What are you doing?" she asked the old woman – she had never seen a spinning wheel before.

The old crone gave a toothless grin. "I'm spinning wool to knit with. Do you want to have a go?"

And she stood up and offered the curious princess a ball of fluffy wool. But as Briar Rose reached over, she somehow over-balanced on her roller-blades and fell forwards, catching her finger on the sharp spindle. Ouch!

She opened her mouth to say something, but all that came out was a giant yawn. By the time she hit the floor, she was already asleep.

The old woman cackled like a crow: "I did it! Now you're dead, *dearest* Briar Rose. Huh! That'll teach the king to ignore me."

Freya, who was in the cake shop when she felt the power of her spell kick in, flew to the palace to warn them all. Briar Rose was carried to her bed and her parents looked over her, anxiously wondering what to do.

"If we have to wait for a hundred years for her to wake, we'll have died of old age," exclaimed the queen in a worried voice.

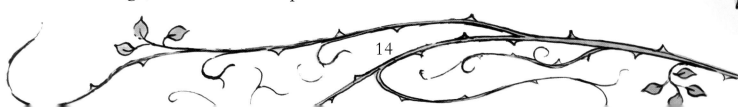

So Freya cast another spell, this time sending the whole palace to sleep until their Princess Rose woke up. As everyone in the whole palace slept, a forest of vicious thorns sprung up around the palace walls to prevent nosy parkers from peeking in.

It was exactly a hundred years later when brave Prince Freddie rode through the forest and noticed a tower sticking up out of the thorny thicket.

"What's hidden in there?" he asked his squire, who asked his servant, who asked a passing farmer.

Naturally when he heard the story of the sleeping princess he couldn't resist a rescue mission – *perhaps he was her true love?* He leapt off his horse and was just about to take his sword to the thorns when an extraordinary thing happened – the thorns parted in front of him. He strode purposefully through the unfriendly prickles and soon arrived at the palace. Everywhere he looked, people were sleeping.

Prince Freddie found Briar Rose lying on her bed surrounded by the snoring courtiers and the king and queen. There was an upward turn to her mouth, making her look so happy, that he couldn't resist stooping down to kiss her.

"What's going on?" asked Briar Rose, sitting bolt upright in surprise.

Of course, it was love at first sight, especially when the prince said he roller-bladed too!

That night, the king organized a surprise party for everyone in the palace. Briar Rose was very over-excited because it wasn't every day that a girl celebrated her 116th birthday, and she and the prince danced far into the night under a blanket of stars.

The biggest surprise, however, was the news that Esmerelda had gone up in smoke when she heard what had happened at the palace. This made the party a safe one as well the happiest one anyone could remember for more than a hundred years.

Sleeping Beauty's Party Invites

If you are going to have a princess party, you will need to ask your friends in a very special way. So get to it and make Sleeping Beauty's sparkling tiara invitations now. Your friends can all wear them to your party to complete their fabulous princess outfits. So let the glitter start here. . . .

Grab a grown-up

A Tiara Fit For A Princess

You will need

A pencil • Tracing paper • Scissors • Gold and silver card • Elastic • Gold and silver pens • Glue • Stick-on jewels • Sequins and glitter • Feathers and fake fur • Envelopes

1. Using your pencil and some tracing paper, place the paper on top of this page and trace round the outline and then cut out the tiara shape. Don't forget to trace the two holes.

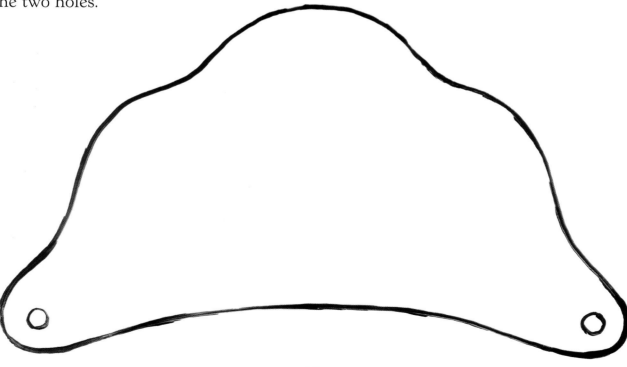

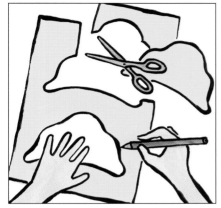

2. Place your tiara shape on a piece of gold or silver card and draw round it. Do this for as many tiaras as you need. When you've done enough, cut the tiara shapes out of the gold card.

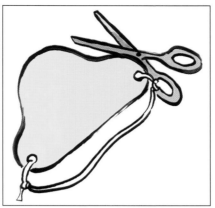

3. Make the two holes at each end of the tiara with the point of your scissors. (Ask a grown-up to help you.) Thread a piece of elastic through one hole tying it with a double knot on the white side of the card.

4. Put the tiara round your head and get someone to thread the elastic through the second hole. Ask a friend to tie it securely on the same side as the other knot. Cut off the elastic that you don't need.

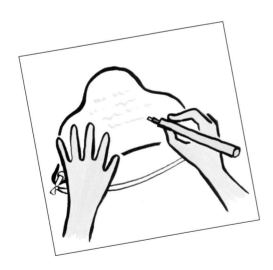

5. Write the party details, like the date, time and where the party is on the white side of the invitation with a gold or silver pen. If you want your friends to come dressed up, write that too.

6. This is where the fun really starts! Turn the tiara over to the gold or silver side and carefully decorate each one differently with stick-on jewels, sequins and glitter. Be really creative!

7. For extra glamour, stick feathers or fake fur on the edge of your tiaras. You can buy fur and feather trims at fabric shops or department stores.

8. When you have finished, place each invitation in an envelope, write the names and addresses and send them to your friends.

Make sure each invitation looks special – a real work of art in its own right and something that all your friends will want to keep as a reminder of a brilliant princess party!

2
The Princess and the Pea

"Darling, you must marry, it's the law – now just look at this picture," wheedled the queen to Prince Julian, passing him a photograph of Princess Passionflower from Somewhere Exotic.

"I won't marry a girl I don't know!" said Julian, striding out of the room and marching upstairs to his bedroom. Why did there have to be a stupid law about him only being able to marry a princess? He lay on his bed and looked up at the ceiling. He thought about his many trips to far-off kingdoms and about how he had danced with hundreds of different princesses: tall, small, fat, thin, white, black, pink – the list was endless. *All he wanted was to meet someone he could truly love – what did it matter if she was a princess or not?* All she had to be was well . . . but that was it, he wouldn't know until he met her. It would take a thunderbolt from the sky to tell him.

Then one dark and stormy night, it happened.

It was Nanny's night off and Prince Julian was in charge of putting his little brother Prince Chester to bed.

"Oooh ooh aah aah! I'm a chimpanzee, come and get me –" laughed the little prince.

"Yes, and I'm Julian of the Jungle and will swing you all the way upstairs to bed if you don't hurry up!"

Suddenly there was a loud knock at the castle door. Unusually, the king went to answer it.

"Those servants do nothing," he grumbled as he heaved the door open. There in the pouring rain stood a beautiful girl, soaked to the skin, her clothes sopping wet and covered in mud.

"Please, can you help me?" pleaded the girl.

"Come in, my dear and stand by the fire. It's far too wet to talk on the doorstep," and the king stepped aside to let the girl in.

At the sound of voices the queen swept into the great hall.

"How can we help you, Miss . . . er?" she said snootily as she took in the girl's sopping clothes and watched the raindrops drip from her nose.

"Princess Daisy, your highness. The propellor of my aeroplane has broken and I'm a long way from home," replied the girl as she curtseyed.

"Hmm, princess you say . . ." murmured the queen. But before she could finish, the kitchen doors burst open and little Prince Chester swung into view, followed by Prince Julian, whooping and beating his chest, wearing nothing but a towel, and closely pursued by an angry cook.

When he caught sight of Daisy, Prince Julian stopped dead – but too late!

CRASH! The cook and he collided! As the cook picked herself up and rushed back to the kitchen, Julian, red-faced, gazed up at the girl before him.

Daisy quickly closed her eyes, trying hard not to laugh. But as the prince scrambled up, his gaze never wavered.

Daisy cautiously opened one eye, taking in the dimple on his right cheek that matched the one on her left, and his chocolate brown eyes that seemed to look right inside her head. It was her turn to blush – he really was very handsome!

"Julian, meet Princess Daisy," said the queen lingering on the word princess and hoping her son would stop staring. But Julian hadn't heard a thing.

"Er," he managed, clutching the towel.

"Hello. . . ." said Daisy. Their eyes met over a pool of rainwater.

But then the queen said briskly, "Daisy, dear, come with me. Let me find you some dry clothes and then you must join us for dinner."

"Uh-ho – it looks like Daisy is going to be put through the wringer," smiled the king.

"Why, because she's so wet?" asked the prince still dazed.

"No! Your mother will be finding out if she's a real princess or not."

"But she says she is!"

"Aha! She may say she's a princess but how do we really know?" replied his father.

"Well, I don't care – and it's too late now. I'm madly in love with her already, whoever she is." And the prince rushed off to get changed.

"So Daisy, where *is* your father's kingdom exactly?" began the queen as she rummaged through her wardrobe for suitable clothes. She needed to know everything. After all, Daisy had to be a proper princess to marry her son.

She continued her probing.

"What would you do if you got spinach in your teeth at a banquet?

"Which fork would you use for spaghetti?

"Do you ride side-saddle?"

All these testing questions and more were fired at poor Daisy who answered them all in a way that seemed to satisfy the queen.

BUT there was one more test that Daisy had to pass after dinner. . . .

As they sat alone after the meal, Daisy and Julian realized they liked the same books (adventure stories), sports (horse riding), food (pizza), and that both of them had broken their legs while climbing trees a long time ago. Julian told Daisy about his travels, far and wide, looking for a bride.

"So you haven't found one yet?" asked Daisy, her heart beating hard.

"I think I have," smiled Julian. "In fact—" but before he could finish, the queen interrupted. *Had she been listening?*

"Daisy, I think I should show you to your room. You look tired."

Not wanting to be rude, Daisy agreed, while the prince fumed silently.

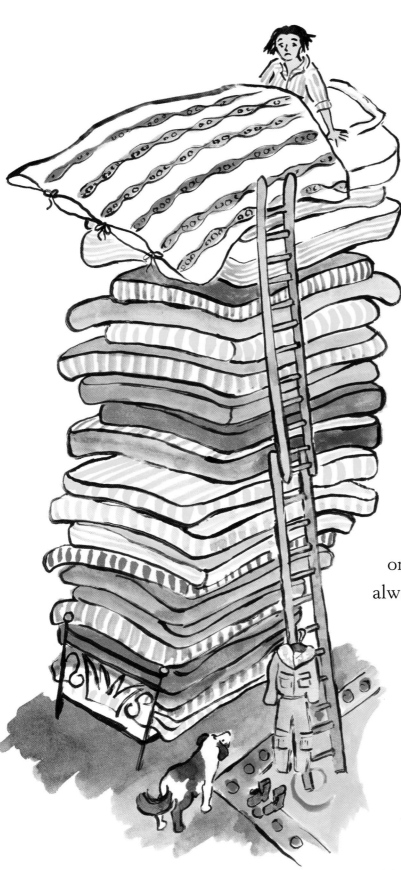

"Oh my!" gasped Daisy as she saw her bed. It was as tall as a haystack and had a ladder up one side so she could get to the top. Twenty mattresses had been piled up on top of each other with a giant eiderdown quilt on top of that.

"Sleep well dear," said the queen, and she slipped quickly out of the door to avoid any questions.

You would have thought that Daisy would have been really cosy with all that cushioning, but she couldn't sleep. It didn't matter where she lay – across the bed, in a star shape, curled up, upside down, on the left or the right – there was always something digging into her back. "Ohhhhhhh!" she screamed in frustration. By morning she was completely dishevelled, tangled up in all the sheets and very cross. Her dimple was glowing pink with anger as she clumped down the ladder, put on her dry clothes and went to breakfast.

"How did you sleep, Daisy?" asked the queen as she poured the tea for the king and Prince Chester.

"Dreadfully!" burst out Daisy, unable to keep it all in. "There was something digging into me all night. Look – I'm covered in bruises!" And she showed her arm, which was, indeed, black and blue.

The queen clapped her hands, dropping the teapot in the process.

"My dear Daisy, it was a pea. I put it under all those mattresses to see if you could feel it, and you did!"

"Mother, have you gone completely batty?" shouted Julian.

"But don't you see," she said, grasping her husband's hand, "this means that Daisy is a real princess – Julian can marry her. Only a real princess would be that sensitive."

"But of course I *am* a real princess!" shouted Daisy, who couldn't believe what she was hearing.

"I don't care if you are or you're not," said Prince Julian. "I love you." And he got down on one knee and proposed there and then.

Daisy didn't say anything for a moment. Everyone held their breath, even Prince Chester who went blue with the effort.

"I will marry you, Prince Julian," she said, "but you will have to ask my father for his permission."

So Julian arrived at Daisy's castle and although he had no idea what was in store for him, he soon found out! There were three princely tests he had to pass: singing "I will always love you," while swinging across a river filled with ferocious piranhas; wrestling with a python as long as a train; and diving from the top of the highest waterfall in the land. Luckily he passed with flying colours, although at the end of the day as he wearily climbed into bed, he slipped and fell, breaking his arm in two places!

30

Soon the day before their wedding arrived and Julian and Daisy managed to escape the hustle and bustle of royal preparation, to steal a few precious moments together.

"Phew, royal weddings are so exhausting!" said Julian. "Oh Daisy darling, do you agree, that when we are married, we should live by our own rules and be happy ever after?"

Daisy smiled, and taking a pen from his top pocket she reached out for his plastered arm. Then she quickly wrote, "I do!"

And so they did and the very next day they waved to the crowds and flew off into a golden sunset.

What Sort of Princess Are You?

Have fun testing each other's qualities with this Party Princess Quiz.

1. You are Sleeping Beauty. No one will explain why you are being kept shut up in the castle till your sixteenth birthday.
Do you:
  a) Break out of the castle any way you can?
  b) Realize there must be a good reason for your captivity and settle down to enjoy life?
  c) Don't bother your pretty little head about it? After all, life as a pampered princess is not that bad!

2. You are Princess Daisy. You've been shown to a room that has a bed with 20 mattresses on it and, unknown to you, there's a pea under the bottom mattress.
Do you:
  a) Become suspicious, search the bed, find the pea, and then snuggle down on one of the mattresses for a good night's sleep?
  b) Think, *How uncomfortable*, as you toss and turn in the bed trying to avoid the lump that keeps on digging into you!
  c) Go straight to sleep and snore loudly all night?

3. You are Beauty. The Beast says you can return home to your father if you promise to go back to him within seven days.
Do you:
  a) Take a horse, briefly pop in at home, before galloping off to freedom?
  b) Visit your father but leave early to get back to the Beast in time?
  c) Promise! What promise?

4. You are Rapunzel. The witch has imprisoned you in the tower.
Do you:

    a) Trick the witch into turning herself into a frog? But OOPS, you're still stuck!

    b) Build a small parachute out of your sheets and escape?

    c) Use the time to try out all the latest hair fashions?

5. You are Snow White. You've got seven dwarves to feed and you can't cook.
Do you:

    a) Find somewhere else to hide?

    b) Look for a cookery book and have fun learning?

    c) Phone for pizza every night?

6. You are Cinderella. Your fairy godmother hasn't turned up.
Do you:

    a) Get even with your stepsisters? Put prickly dust in their clothes!

    b) Raid your stepsisters' cast offs, create your own special look and then go to the ball?

    c) Make a bucket of popcorn and slump in front of the television?

How did you do?

Mostly 'a's. You are Princess Impulsive! You know what you want and no one gets in your way! How about thinking a little before you act? Everybody should be considerate, even if they've been unfairly treated.

Mostly 'b's. Hello Princess Perfect! You are kind-hearted, intelligent and loving. But don't take yourself too seriously – every now and then let your tiara slip a little and have some fun!

Mostly 'c's. You are Princess In-Need-Of-Training! As well as sparkling on the outside, start developing those qualities of loyalty, love and laughter. In no time, you'll be a princess through and through!

The Ultimate Princess Test

Now it's time for the most important test of all. . . . At your next sleepover party, place a dried pea under each mattress or sleeping bag and see who is the most sensitive.

Which one of you is the real princess – or maybe you all are!

3
Beauty and
the Beast

"The Beast! The Beast! We've all got to hide!" cried Joseph, as he crashed through the door and fell to the stone floor, clutching a perfect red rose. Beauty, Hope and Charity, his daughters, jumped up and ran to him.

"You should have seen his face! Those fangs, yellow eyes and claws – it was hideous!" he jabbered.

"Who on earth are you talking about?" asked Charity, terrified.

"Father, just tell us," said Beauty, handing him a glass of water.

Joseph sat down, took a deep breath and tried to collect his thoughts. Could it really be only yesterday that he got caught in that terrible storm on his way home from the city?

"I was lost in the forest and found myself at the gates of an enormous castle. I walked up to the front door which stood open. I was so cold and wet that I went inside. I called and called but no one answered. In the dining room, I found a huge table piled with food. I realized I was hungry, so I sat down and ate." He paused for breath.

"Next door, I found a bed and as I was exhausted I lay down to rest – and fell asleep until morning. When I woke up, I dressed as quickly as I could and started to leave." He paused again to sip his water.

"And . . ." cried his daughters in unison.

"And, as I was leaving the castle grounds I passed a rose garden. I'd bought presents for Hope and Charity but hadn't found anything for you, Beauty, so I stole a single red rose."

He dropped the flower, shivering at the memory. "The Beast came from nowhere and knocked me to the ground. I thought he was going to kill me for taking it and I begged him to spare my life. He did, but, in return, I had to promise to bring the kindest of my daughters to the castle to live with him – for ever!"

"Wh-which one of us is that, Father?" squeaked Charity, her bottom lip trembling.

"Beauty. . . ." breathed Joseph.

It was a month later, and Beauty sat alone in her tower bedroom in the Beast's castle. She had insisted that her father kept his promise and had duly arrived at the castle with her suitcase packed – for good. . . .

Since then she had rarely seen the Beast, and though fearful of him she now felt restless and lonely. She decided to pluck up courage to explore the castle even though this had been expressly forbidden. In no time, she found herself standing in a large, neglected room. All around her lay torn and ripped paintings of a handsome young man and heaps of dust-covered designer men's clothes. On the far wall, Beauty caught sight of an oval mirror, sparkling like a bubbling spring – she felt strangely drawn to it.

"What do you wish to see?" it gurgled secretly to her.

Beauty jumped – a talking mirror?

"My family," she replied in an instant, not knowing what to expect. The mirror dissolved, then cleared, and Beauty could see her father sitting by the fire in their little cottage, talking sadly to her sisters. She leaned closer to listen to what he was saying.

"But it has been a month since she left and we have still heard nothing. I am sick with worry," her father said weakly.

"Oh Father, don't blame yourself. Beauty insisted you kept your promise," said Hope as she comforted him while Charity stroked his hand.

Beauty felt tears prick her eyes and she reached out to touch the glass. But at that very moment, the image faded, and Beauty saw the Beast's terrifying reflection in the mirror behind her own.

"What do you think you are doing?" he roared. "I told you NEVER to come here and you have deliberately disobeyed me." He shook with rage and brought his huge hairy face close to hers. He stared deep into her eyes with his big, bloodshot ones and his breath singed her eyebrows.

Beauty felt faint from fright but she took a deep breath and replied, "I-I-I . . . I'm so lonely! I have no friends and I miss my family." Then, as she felt her courage return, she cried, "Why do you keep me here? You never want to see me and when you do, we never talk. All you do is demand that I marry you. Why should I marry you? Why should I even like you? You're bossy and beastly – you never wash and your breath stinks."

39

Beauty was surprised by her outburst but no more so than the Beast. At first she thought he might kill her with a single swipe of his massive paw. But then his face crumpled and he shrunk back, almost as if hurt.

"I am sorry you feel like that. If I have avoided you, I apologize. I thought it only best to . . . oh, what's the use. I can't explain. Don't ever come in here again!" And he stumbled out, barging into furniture and banging his head on the door.

In an instant kind-hearted Beauty felt sorry for him. She ran to the door – but he had gone.

Later that evening, as Beauty brushed her teeth, she heard a knock at the door. The Beast was standing there. He looked different. He had brushed his mane and his teeth looked less yellow. In his paw, he carried a pair of golden tweezers.

"I wonder," he said gruffly, "if you could help? I have a thorn in my hand."

Beauty hesitated. Then she smiled gently and invited him in. As she helped him, they began to talk. She told him about her life and her family. He entertained her with wonderful stories about places and people she had only dreamed of.

The next morning, Beauty woke up to find a gift box, bound in ribbon, outside her room. Inside, sprinkled with petals and wrapped in layers of glittering tissue were rose-scented soaps and bottles of bubble bath. She was thrilled. In spite of her name, nobody had ever made a fuss of her. But what Beauty wanted most of all was to see the Beast again. Could it be that he was just lonely too?

And from that moment on, Beauty and the Beast enjoyed their time together – they had fun! But it wasn't to last long and their happiness evaporated with the morning dew, on the day of her father's birthday. Beauty woke up as usual but instead of looking forward to the day ahead she felt listless and homesick.

"I know what I can do to help you," the Beast said, sighing deeply, and he took her to the room with the magic mirror. It was as if he could feel her sadness.

"I wish to see my father," Beauty whispered to the mirror. Soon, Joseph appeared in the glass but to her horror, he looked white and feverish, with Charity mopping his brow.

"Oh Father!" gasped Beauty and with a sob she ran from the room, all the way through the castle until she reached the rose garden. And that was where the Beast found her, in their favourite place. In his hand he carried her coat and suitcase.

"Here, you will need these if you are to visit home," he growled softly.

She looked up at him with tears in her eyes.

"You mean I can go?" she asked.

"Not forever. You must return in seven days or I will . . ." He turned his head away miserably.

41

Six days after Beauty had returned home, her father recovered. Her sisters were pleased to see Beauty although they were a little jealous of her glowing complexion and her shining eyes – she looked just like a princess. And everything about life with the Beast seemed to smell of roses!

Each day Beauty cooked her father nourishing soup and helped her sisters about the house. But every evening, her thoughts would turn to the Beast, back at the castle. This was the time of day she missed him most. She remembered how they would chat about everything under the sun, make plans for the next day or just sit quietly in the garden. The only thing he would never discuss was why he never left his home.

On the seventh day, Beauty woke up with butterflies in her stomach. She was so looking forward to seeing the Beast!

"Oh stay one more day, please?" Hope begged. "Father will miss you so much and I'm afraid he isn't well enough yet." Beauty thought hard. *Surely another day would make no difference to the Beast?*

On the eighth day, just before dawn, Beauty returned to the castle. It was still dark and raining heavily as Beauty splashed through the puddles in her special golden Wellington boots. As she ran in the front door, she shook off her coat and cried, "Yoo-hoo, Beast, I'm home!" But there was no answer. "Where are you? I've made you some fudge!" She searched every nook and cranny but couldn't find him anywhere.

The mirror will show me, she thought and she sped to the forbidden room.

"I wish to see the Beast," she cried. The mirror fizzed and sparkled before dissolving to show the rose garden, and there, sprawled on the ground, lay the Beast!

Beauty shrieked in horror, and before the image had faded
she had run out into the garden – the rain lashing her face.

He was breathing – but only just.

"Beast, please forgive me, I am so sorry that I am late."
As he lay there motionless, she took his paw in her hands.

"I'll never leave you again, please don't die. I'll do anything."

His lips moved. Beauty leaned forward, breathing
in the comforting smell of his damp fur.

"Will you marry me?" he croaked.
The effort made him cough.

"Yes, I will," she breathed, closing
her eyes to the stinging rain.

And then it happened. It stopped pouring – the clouds vanished, rosebuds unfurled and the sun came up! Beauty opened her eyes and to her surprise saw that the Beast had gone! Instead, sitting in front of her, patting her hand, was a smiling young man – handsome, dark haired and green-eyed!

"Where's the Beast? What have you done to him?" she snapped, snatching her hand away.

"Beauty, don't you recognize me?" he asked.

She looked stunned – his voice sounded so familiar. . . .

"My name is Casper, Prince Casper," he said and he told her his story. An evil enchantress had cursed him by turning him into a beast for refusing to marry her. As she cast her spell, she had laughed out loud and said he had a year to find a wife or he would die – ugly and alone! Beauty had returned just in time.

"Will you marry me?" he asked again, looking nervous. "I've loved you since I first saw you."

Beauty narrowed her eyes and grinned. "Yes, although you're a little too handsome for my liking!"

And so, later that afternoon, Beauty married her Beast.

And she carried in her hand a single, red rose – after all that's how their story began!

Beauty's Beauty Tips

Do you feel like turning your friends into real beauty princesses?
Settle down in front of a huge collection of glitter and gloss and get
ready for lots of sparkle and giggles. But don't forget, beauty is more
than just skin deep. Being kind and caring to everybody is as important
– just like Beauty!

Smelling of Roses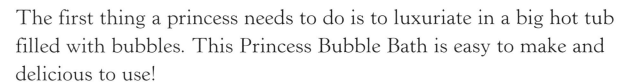

The first thing a princess needs to do is to luxuriate in a big hot tub
filled with bubbles. This Princess Bubble Bath is easy to make and
delicious to use!

You will need

300 ml of unscented liquid soap • 100 ml of distilled water (available from
supermarkets) • 14 drops of rose oil or any favourite oil • 2 drops of pink food
colouring to make it look pretty • Small empty plastic bottles with screw tops

Put all the ingredients into a bowl and mix well. Carefully pour the mixture into
bottles and hey presto – instant bubble bath!

Princess Sparkle Gel

To shine like a true princess, a little glitter worn carefully should do the trick, so why not follow this simple recipe for home-made glitter gel?

You will need

Clear aloe vera gel (You can buy this from most chemists. Is is used as an after sun soother.) • Glitter (Make sure you buy the stuff for cosmetic use and not the glitter for sprinkling on cards!) • A pretty screw-top jar to keep your glitter in

1. Empty the gel into a bowl and sprinkle in as much glitter as you want.

2. Mix thoroughly and then carefully decant the mixture into the jar.

3. Put glitter everywhere that you want to twinkle like a star!

★ TOP TIP ★ If you are going to put glitter on your face, be very careful not to get it anywhere near your eyes.

Princess Body Make-Up

To create cute pictures on your
body with jewels and make up, try this:

* Either copy one of these pictures of a dolphin, moon, flower,
sun, butterfly and star – or find something else you like – on to a
piece of stiff card, then cut it out. Using a body paint, get a
friend to draw round this on to your tummy, arm, shoulder, back etc.
Fill in the outline with eye shadow or body paint.

* Another idea is to do a design that fits round your belly button
and then show it off in a cropped T-shirt. Add sequins round the
design using clear lip-gloss, or Vaseline to stick them in place.

* Instead of wearing bracelets and rings, make intricate patterns
on your wrists and fingers with sequins stuck on with lip-gloss
or Vaseline.

4
Rapunzel

49

"What do you think you're doing, stealing my herbs?" screeched a voice that sounded like nails scraping down a blackboard.

Jack turned round. He hadn't noticed that the door to the cottage behind him had opened. A bent figure shuffled towards him, rollers in her hair and a pipe in her tight-lipped mouth.

"I should turn you into a statue right now," she hissed. Jack looked for a way to escape, but his legs wouldn't move. She was a witch and he was under a spell.

"Please don't turn me to stone, I'll do anything," Jack begged. "We've just moved next door and my wife has been desperate for some rampion ever since she spotted it in your garden – she refuses to eat anything else and is fading away. I'm frightened she'll die."

"So, you'll do anything?" the witch asked. Jack nodded eagerly.

"Right," cackled the old woman, "your wife is expecting a baby daughter. I want her for my own!"

Jack felt torn in two. At first he was elated – he and his wife had hoped for a child for years and at last they were going to be blessed with a baby. But then he felt crushed at the thought of giving the child away to this old hag. All he could do was hope that she was wrong and that they would have a boy instead.

Hannah cried with joy when she discovered she was carrying a child. She didn't care if she had a son or a daughter, but Jack prayed with all his might for a boy. His wife still craved rampion, and every day the witch left a fresh bunch of it on their doorstep.

Finally, the big day arrived. Jack was so terrified of the witch that he locked all the doors and windows to their little house. As he held his wife's hand, the midwife announced the baby was a girl. Hannah reached out to hold her baby, but before she could, two claw-like hands snatched the child away.

"My daughter!" cried Hannah.

"No, *my* daughter, and I shall call her Rapunzel," said the witch, and she twirled her cloak about her and the baby and disappeared from their lives in the blink of an eye.

Ten years had passed since that fateful day. The witch now lived in a cottage far away from any neighbours and Rapunzel was forbidden to go to school or to make any friends. The witch wanted to keep her all to herself.

"Stop that now!" the old crone hissed.

Rapunzel was practising back-flips in the mud, covering herself in the process! Only her golden hair, worn in two long plaits, shone as she landed perfectly with a huge smile on her face.

"Yes, Mother," Rapunzel sighed, realizing she'd been caught in the act, again.

"I thought I told you to go inside to sew patches on those massive holes you made in your dress yesterday."

"But if you'd let me wear trousers instead of silly frilly dresses, then I wouldn't tear them, would I?"

"Not another word – go inside and get sewing. I've run you a bath – little ladies don't smell like cow pats!" croaked the witch.

Rapunzel hated wearing dresses, she hated not being able to play with other children and, most of all, she hated her hair – why she had to have it so long was beyond her, but her mother always insisted.

"One day your beauty and your hair will be the making of you, my girl," was all she would say each time Rapunzel begged for the scissors.

But Rapunzel wanted to be famous for her talent, not her beauty. She longed to run away and join the circus, so she could do back-flips and juggle flaming batons all day long!

As the years zoomed by, Rapunzel blossomed from a tom-boyish, skinny child into a beautiful young woman. Her hair was now too long to wear loose and, when she didn't have it plaited, she kept it wound up on top of her head. She still hated it though, and she still dreamed of joining the circus.

"I have a surprise for you, my dear," said the witch one day.

It was Rapunzel's sixteenth birthday. As she plaited her hair she looked at the witch excitedly.

"At last!" said Rapunzel. "Let me guess. It's a visit to Amazing Aldo's Travelling Circus! I know they are near here at the moment. I can hear the elephants calling!"

The witch didn't answer but blindfolded her daughter instead.

Rapunzel felt uneasy; something wasn't right. They left the cottage and the witch led her by the hand deep into the woods.

Eventually they stopped and the witch whipped off the girl's blindfold. Rapunzel blinked in the bright light. In front of her stood a dazzling gothic tower made entirely of gold – taller than the highest tree. There was a tiny window at the top, but no other way in. Tangled roses grew at the foot of the tower, unable to grow up the shiny gold bricks.

"This is for you, Daughter," said the witch. "Happy birthday."

"But what. . . ?" Rapunzel felt sick and dizzy but before she could finish her question, she'd fainted. . . .

A room swam into focus. It was circular and decorated in purple polka dots – which she HATED.

"Mother!" she shouted.

"Yes," came a distant voice from far below.

Rapunzel leapt to the window and looked down at the witch.

"Why am I up here – I can't get out!"

"Hang your hair out of the window and I'll climb up your plait and tell you," replied the witch.

Rapunzel did just that, securing it on a curtain hook at the side to stop it from pulling too hard. Soon the witch was hauling herself up the tower, through the window and into the room.

"Rapunzel, you know how precious you are to me," cooed the old crone. "I just want you to have the best things in life, and become the most famous beauty in all the land." And she smiled a gummy smile.

"Well, I won't! I'll escape! I shall run away and join the circus!"

The witch looked at her in a way that made Rapunzel shut up at once.

"You won't escape because you can't – the only way in and out is by your hair. I suggest you get used to your new home." And she stroked Rapunzel's head affectionately.

"At this rate I'll never find the Amazing Aldo's Travelling Circus. It'll have moved on," said Prince Harry to his long-suffering horse, Galahad. They were lost in the woods and just as they were about to go round in another circle, he heard a sad lilting song.

"What a beautiful voice," he gasped. He followed the sound all the way to a clearing where he stared up at an extraordinary golden tower before him. He could see no way in or out but he knew the voice was coming from inside. Prince Harry was so enraptured that he settled down to wait for the singer to appear.

"Rapunzel, Rapunzel, let down your long hair."
It was the next morning, and the prince woke with a jump at the sound of an old woman's voice. He was just in time to see a long golden plait tumble from the window of the tower. Then he watched in disbelief as an old hag climbed up it and disappeared inside. He waited patiently all day. When evening came, the plait was let down again and the woman slithered to the ground and hobbled off into the trees opposite.

The prince ran to the foot of the tower and, imitating the old woman's voice called, "Rapunzel, Rapunzel, let down your long hair." Sure enough, the plait was thrown down and the prince seizing his chance, began to climb up.

"You're not my mother!" shrieked Rapunzel as Prince Harry appeared at the window.

"Please don't be angry," he said. "I heard your singing and had to meet you. Are you an enchanted princess in need of rescuing?"

Rapunzel burst out laughing. "No, I'm just Rapunzel but I do need saving. Who are you?"

"I'm Prince Harry. But, if you're not a princess, why are you locked in this tower?" Rapunzel told him all about it over tea and biscuits.

"As you see, I'm trapped. I've tried making ladders out of my clothes, but my mother always finds them before I've finished making them. The only thing strong enough to hold me is a rope of my hair, but it's on my head and I haven't any scissors!"

The more they talked, the more they liked each other. Then Rapunzel showed him her juggling and told him how she wanted to join the circus.

Prince Harry couldn't believe it. He'd run away because he wanted to join a circus too – being a prince was just so dull! They talked all night, planning a double act and how they would wow the crowds with their dazzling tricks.

57

As sunlight slowly crept into the tower the prince leapt to his feet.

"This is barmy," he said. "I'm going to fetch my sword. We'll cut off your hair and then we can use it to escape."

But Rapunzel said, "No, it's too late now. It's morning and Mother will be here in a minute. Come back this evening, it will be safer then."

Sure enough, the prince just made it to the trees as the witch scuttled into the clearing and began climbing up Rapunzel's hair.

Up in the tower, Rapunzel felt the familiar tugging and without thinking she cried crossly, "Come on, Mother, why do you take so much longer than the prince . . . OOPS!"

"What?!" The witch went berserk. She pulled out a huge pair of scissors and with a curse, began muttering a magic spell. In a flash, the plait slipped to the floor.

Suddenly, Rapunzel felt herself spin in the air, but it wasn't a velvet carpet she fell onto – it was sand! She was all alone in the wilderness, sitting outside a cave – her feet shackled to a rock by long golden chains.

Later that evening, the witch lay in wait for the prince in the tower.

"Rapunzel, Rapunzel, let down your long hair," called out the prince. The rope of hair was let down. But when he climbed up it and saw the old hag, he was horrified.

"Where's Rapunzel? What have you done to her?" he shouted.

"She's gone and you'll never see her again!" screeched the witch cackling madly – and she pushed him out of the window.

As the prince fell, he lunged at the old woman and together they tumbled to the ground, the prince landing on top of the witch – killing her instantly. He was alive but totally blinded – the thorns on the roses had pierced his eyes. He wandered helplessly around the clearing until Galahad found him.

"We've got to find her," Prince Harry whispered to his faithful horse as he slumped in the saddle.

After months of searching far and wide, and just as the prince was about to give up, he heard the same lilting song he'd heard long ago in the forest. He couldn't believe his ears. He and Gallahad set off to follow the sound, their feet not touching the ground until they reached the cave where Rapunzel was imprisoned. Rapunzel stared up at the blind man on his horse. Like her, his clothes and his hair were ragged and torn.

"Prince Harry! Can it be you?" Rapunzel asked breathlessly.

"Yes, oh yes!" cried Harry throwing himself off his horse and into her arms. She cried with joy at seeing him. When they kissed, her tears touched his eyes, and in an instant, they were healed!

Prince Harry could see again!

"My poor love," he whispered when he saw her ragged clothes, her cropped hair and her sunburnt skin. "What did that old witch do to you?"

Rapunzel looked down at her rags and at the chains around her ankles. "This is nothing," she said, shuffling back into the cave.

"Look at what else my dear mother did to me." And Rapunzel pointed to a shelf of dusty, well-thumbed books about circus tricks and a set of juggling balls – all out of reach, and meant to taunt her.

"She knew that this was worse than any punishment she could give me."

"But Rapunzel," said Harry, "now we can use these things to plan our circus act together!" And with one clean blow, he severed her chains with his sword. She was free at last!

"I was thinking," Rapunzel said a little while later, "we should start with juggling batons of fire before I teach you how to do forward somersaults and back-flips!"

"We can do whatever you want," said Harry. "As long as I am with you, I shall be happy!"

And so Rapunzel and Harry made plans for the greatest royal circus show on earth. And from that day forward, Rapunzel wore her hair short and spiky and together they juggled their way to happiness.

Hair by Rapunzel

Grab a grown-up

Does your long hair drive you crazy hanging like limp curtains! Why not adopt the Rapunzel solution (before the wicked witch cut all her hair off) and get plaiting!

The Fabulous French Plait -

1. It's easier to do this plait if your hair is a little bit damp! Begin by placing your hands slightly behind your ears and draw them back and upwards to the crown of your head, gathering a small amount of hair as you go.

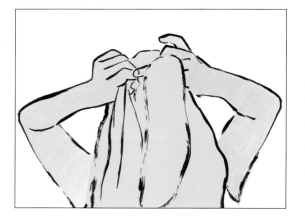

2. Divide the hair you are holding into three small sections and do one plait by crossing the left strand over the centre strand (i.e these two strands change places) and then complete the plait by crossing the right strand over the centre.

3. Hold the plait in your right hand, keeping the three strands separate. Place your left hand behind your left ear again and draw up a strand of hair, half as thick as the original strand. Add this to the left strand of the original plait and cross this increased section over to the centre.

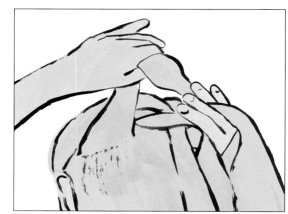

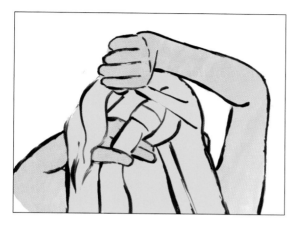

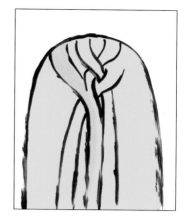

4. Now hold the plait in your left hand, keeping the three strands separate. Place your right hand behind your right ear and draw up a strand of hair, half as thick as the original strand. Add this to the right strand of the original plait and cross the increased section over to the centre.

5. Continue gathering the hair from the left and right and adding it to the plait.

6. When you get to the end of the hair, fasten the plait with a band. Add press-on hair jewels to the hair for that extra fairy-tale princess look!

★ TOP TIP ★ Strangely enough it's easier to do a French plait yourself, if you DON'T look in the mirror!

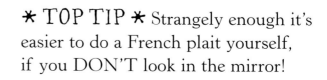

Rough with the Smooth

After Rapunzel had all her hair hacked off, she could have done with a style like this to jazz up those shorn locks.

1. Brush your hair well and then carefully divide your hair into two sections across your head from ear to ear.

2. Part the front half in the centre. Put some gloss on and curl the bits by your ears into kiss curls.

3. Secure your parting with jewelled clips. Slick gel into the back of your hair and back-comb and scrunch so it stands up.

Very funky princesses!

5
Snow White

"What? I don't believe it! No one is more beautiful than I," raged the queen, knocking a golden pot of face cream to the floor of her castle boudoir. She turned to her magic mirror and asked once more.

"Mirror, mirror on the wall,
Who is the fairest of them all?"
The mirror shivered and replied,
"You my queen are fair, it's true,
But Snow White has grown more fair than you!"

The queen paled. "Fetch me the huntsman!" she snarled to her maid. Snow White was the queen's unlucky stepdaughter. Her father the king had died many years ago leaving her to the care of her stepmother. Over the years, Snow White had grown from a gawky girl into a beautiful young princess – too beautiful for the vain and wicked queen.

The huntsman knocked at her door. "Your majesty, you called?"

The queen sat filing her nails, which were long and pointed like the talons of a bird of prey and dipped in crimson polish. Without looking up she spoke, her voice colder than an arctic frost.

"Take Snow White deep into the forest and get rid of her!"

"B-b-but your majesty. . . ." the huntsman stuttered.

"Do not fail me – and I shall want proof!" And she dismissed him with a flick of her finger.

"Snow White, run as fast as you can," urged the huntsman, unable to finish his terrible task. A shocked and bewildered Snow White fled into the dark forest ahead.

"She's dead, your Majesty," the huntsman reported a few hours later, handing the queen a bag containing the heart of an unlucky boar that had skidded across his path on the way back to the castle. The queen peered inside, her almond eyes narrowing, her rosebud mouth puckering unpleasantly.

"Hmm, feed it to the hounds!" she said disinterestedly, reaching for her scarlet lip-gloss.

"Ouch! Ow! Bother!" cried Snow White as she ran tripping through the trees, brambles catching her hair and scratching her marble-white skin.

"How am I ever going to find a way out of this forest?" she despaired.

She struggled on for a while before falling over a tree stump and landing flat on her face in some rabbit droppings. When she looked up she saw, to her delight, a tiny cottage in the fading evening light. The thorny bushes had hidden it from view.

Snow White picked herself up and walked up to the front door. She knocked loudly.

"Hello! Is anybody home?" she called. When nobody answered, she pushed open the door and crept inside. "Ouch," she cried banging her head on a very low ceiling. In front of her she spied a narrow staircase.

"I'm so tired," she thought, "I wonder if there's somewhere upstairs where I could rest?" The stairs led to a little room in the roof and there, in a row, stood seven tiny beds. They were all much too small for her so she lay across three of them.

"I'll just close my eyes for a moment," she yawned and promptly fell asleep. She didn't hear the door slam. . . .

"Wake up. Wake up!" At the sound of voices Snow White sat bolt upright, banging her head on a beam again.

"Where am I?" she cried, fumbling blindly around in the darkness.

"Hurry up and turn your lamps on, so she can see us," said a gruff voice. Seven friendly faces peered down at her.

"Who are you?" they all cried together.

The faces belonged to seven dwarves who listened carefully to Snow White as she told them all about her evil stepmother.

"So she told the huntsman to kill me, but he freed me and I just ran and ran. I have nowhere else to go," she ended sadly. The little men stood in a huddle, murmuring to themselves and glancing up at Snow White. After a pause, they asked, "Can you cook?"

"Well, not really, I've been a princess all my life but I can learn pretty quickly!" said Snow White with a smile that would have melted even the frostiest of hearts.

And so, she stayed and cooked for her new-found friends. At first it was beans on toast until she got to grips with the stove. But the dwarves didn't mind – they loved her and she loved them. Snow White always looked forward to the end of the day when they would troop through the door after work and wolf down all the sweets and cakes, and pastries and pancakes, she had made for them all day long. Some days there was so much food left over that they occasionally thought of opening a little tea-shop – after all, the dwarves weren't getting any younger.

Back at the castle, the queen smiled cruelly into her magic mirror. With a wave of her wand of mascara, she said smugly,

"Mirror, mirror on the wall,
Now who's the fairest of them all?"
But the mirror paused and quivered,
"*You my queen, are fair, it's true,
But Snow White is still more fair than you!*"

"What! My stepdaughter lives?" The queen screeched, dropping her powder puff in horror. "Well, we'll soon see about that!"
And with a shriek, she whirled around her darkened chamber collecting her magic potions. She mixed them in a pot until a choking green smoke filled the air.

70

Then, she took a red apple from her fruit bowl and held it up to the mirror on the wall.

"See this apple – it will kill her!" she coughed, and dipped it in the pot, coating it with her evil magic.

The queen then disguised herself as an old peddler woman and with a cry of, "Bon appétit!" she put the apple in a basket and shuffled off to seek out Snow White.

"Don't work too hard!" teased Snow White, waving the dwarves off to work before returning indoors, eager to begin her cooking. Today she was planning to make toffee apples! As she gathered her things, she noticed that Norvig, her favourite dwarf, had forgotten his lunch box. "Never mind, he'll be back," she smiled and carried on with her task.

She was so absorbed that she didn't hear the door creak open.

"Mmmm, what a lovely smell!"

Snow White jumped. An old peddler woman was standing behind her.

"Can I help you?" asked Snow White, wondering why she was suddenly covered in goose bumps.

"There's no need to be startled, my dear. I was passing and wondered if you wanted to buy some of my lovely, red apples?" said the old woman.

"Well, I am making toffee apples . . . but I have plenty already," Snow White replied politely. "But look how juicy they are," coaxed the crone.

For a second, Snow White felt dizzy. She closed her eyes and could almost imagine the taste of delicious, sweet, caramelized toffee fused with the tart, crunchiness of apple. She opened her eyes and smiled. Then she reached out her hand to the basket and picked out the rosiest apple. She put it to her lips, took a bite and . . . fell to the floor!

"Hah! Now who's the most gorgeous girl in the world!" squawked the queen throwing off her filthy hag rags.

"What have you done to Snow White?" a voice suddenly shouted. The queen whipped round. It was Norvig – he had come back for his lunch. "The queen!" he shuddered. Anger flooded his veins, and before the queen could arch an eyebrow, Norvig had lifted his axe and felled her with a single blow. Then seeing Snow White, he sat down on the front step and sobbed as if his heart would break.

When the rest of the dwarves returned home, they were so sad that they cried for days. When they recovered they realized winter was approaching. The dwarves couldn't bear to bury Snow White in the cold, damp ground so they made her a beautiful bed inside a glass case. But it was too big for the cottage so it had to rest outside instead.

As the days shortened, and the flowers faded in the garden, the dwarves noticed to their surprise that Snow White's beauty remained unchanged. Her cheeks were still tinged with rose, her dark hair still shone, and her lips were as red as holly berries. It was if she was simply asleep. Each morning, as they went off to work they would blow her a kiss as they passed.

One freezing day, a prince came riding by. He was lost in the forest and his horse was struggling through the snow. Seeing a glow in the distance, he dismounted and leading his horse, he followed the light all the way to a little cottage garden. There, to his surprise, he found a glass case, shining in the snow. Inside was the most beautiful girl he had ever seen, and she was fast asleep!

He leant forward to touch the glass – it warmed his hands. He gazed at the girl, hypnotized by her beauty. It was as if she had led him to her.

The prince walked up to the cottage door.

He knocked loudly but there was no answer although the door was slightly ajar. He was so cold that he decided to shelter from the snow but he couldn't just leave the girl alone outside. Trudging back through the snow he knelt down by the glass case and gently lifted the lid. Then he reached inside and took the girl in his arms. She felt as light as a feather and smelt of toffee and apples! He was about to carry her back to the cottage when he heard the crunch of footsteps behind him.

"What do you think you are doing?" seven angry voices cried in unison.

Startled, the prince slipped on some ice, and to his horror, he dropped the girl into a pile of snow!

"Ugh!" said Snow White spitting out a lump of poisoned apple. "That's better. Now why am I sitting in a snowdrift?" She looked around her, a smile lighting her face.

The dwarves couldn't believe their eyes and nor could the prince. Snow White turned to him. "Who are you?" she said, suddenly feeling shy.

"I'm Crown Prince Alexander, and I was lost until I found you!"

"Well," laughed Snow White, "you must be very hungry if you've travelled from afar. Come on everybody, let's go inside and I'll make us something good to eat."

 SNOW WHITE

And so they all trooped into the little house. Snow White and her prince fell in love over steaming mugs of hot cocoa – and delicious marzipan swirls.

As for the seven dwarves, in time they retired, and set up a little tea-shop for lost and weary travellers. They served sweets and cakes, pastries and pancakes – all by royal appointment!

Snow White's Party Bites

A princess has got to eat, so try making these yummy delights for your party. If Snow White can so can you!

Grab a grown-up

Mini Potato Cheese Pancakes

You will need

1 egg • 1 teaspoon milk • 1 large potato, grated • 75g grated Cheddar cheese • 1 tablespoon flour • Salt and pepper • Oil or butter, for frying

1. Whisk the egg and mix in the milk, grated potato, cheese, flour, and finally add salt and pepper to taste. If the mixture is too stiff to drop off the spoon easily, add a little extra milk.

2. Ask a grown-up to heat a frying pan with a little oil or butter and drop spoonfuls of the mixture in the pan. They should spread out like mini pancakes. If not, press them down with a spoon.

3. Cook the pancakes until they are brown on both sides and serve hot or cold. You can spread them with cream cheese, pâté, sour cream or any other topping, but they are also yummy on their own.

Toffee Apples – the easy microwave way

You will need

8 small apples washed and dried • 225 ml water •
450g sugar • Eight 10cm wooden craft sticks

Grab a grown-up

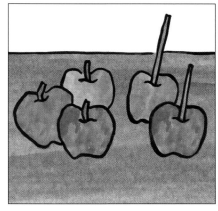

1. Put the sugar and water into a glass bowl and cook uncovered on Full Power for 2 minutes. Remove and stir until sugar has dissolved completely. Watching carefully, continue cooking on Full Power until syrup is golden in colour.

2. Meanwhile, wash and dry the apples. Then twist off their stems and push a stick firmly into each one. When the toffee mixture has finished cooking, take it very carefully out of the microwave and let it stand for 2 minutes.

3. Now carefully dip the apples into the toffee, using a spoon to cover them all over. Remember the mixture will be very hot. Hold the apples over the bowl to drain them and then stand on greaseproof paper to let the toffee harden.

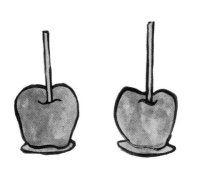

Marzipan Swirls

You will need

One block of readymade marzipan • One packet of puff pastry •
Jam – any flavour you fancy! • Greased baking sheet

Grab a grown-up

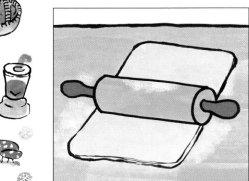  

1. Preheat the oven to 230 C/450 F/Gas Mark 8. Roll out the pastry on a floured surface till it is about 3mm thick. Roll the marzipan till it is the same size as the pastry.

2. Lay the marzipan on top of the pastry. Spread the jam of your choice over the marzipan, then roll the slab into a sausage shape. Chill in the fridge for one hour.

3. Slice the sausage into thin discs and place on a greased baking sheet. Pop in the oven for about 10 minutes until the pastry has risen and is nice and golden.

What a feast for a gaggle of princesses!

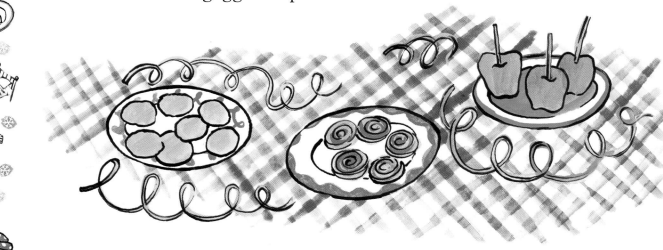

6
Cinderella

It was a sunny morning in September when a gold envelope flopped on to the doormat. Cinderella took it through to the dining room where her weasel-faced stepsisters were slouching.

"Hand me that letter at once," screeched Camilla, the elder of the two stepsisters, when she saw the royal red seal.

"It's an invitation to a ball at the royal palace on Saturday. It's from the prince and it says that all the ladies of the house are invited!"

Cinderella caught her breath. *All the ladies* – that meant her too, but she knew better than to ask if she could go: the answer would most certainly be *No*. She thought sadly about how happy she had been when her father was alive. But as soon as he had died, her terrible stepmother had made her sleep in the dark and dusty attic, and forced her to do all the housework. But what was the use in being bitter and angry? At least she had a roof over her head, didn't she?

"I'll wear my purple dress with the big bow," crowed Camilla, breaking through Cinderella's thoughts.

"You'll look terrible – *I* want to wear purple!" sniped her grouchy sister, Clarissa. The bickering continued all week, with Cinderella running here and there after everyone, picking up dresses from shops and collecting shoes from the cobbler. Finally the day of the ball arrived. The sisters were shouting from one room or another: "Cinderella, come and tie my corset!" "Cinderella, I need my toenails cutting!" "Cinderella, brush my hair!" until at last it was time for them to go to the prince's ball.

"You must clean the whole house from top to bottom before we come home. You've let the housework slide this week," her stepmother snapped as they were leaving.

"But—" Cinderella started to protest and was immediately silenced with an icy glare.

"Oh yes, the coal cellar needs scrubbing, too!" added Clarissa. The two stepsisters sniggered at each other, looking just like a couple of trolls.

And with that order ringing in Cinderella's ears, they were gone.

Cinderella sat down at the bottom of the stairs. She felt like screaming. She put her beautiful face in her hands and a tear slid down her cheek. She wished for the millionth time that she could have gone to the ball. . . .

"Ahem! Is that what you wish for, my dear?" spoke a voice in her ear.

Cinderella jumped to her feet and gasped. Standing before her was a beautiful woman with a feather in her hair.

"Who are you?" asked Cinderella. "How did you read my mind?"

"It's my job to know your wishes; I am your fairy godmother. So you want to go to the ball?"

Cinderella nodded, dumbstruck. *Since when did she have a fairy godmother?*

"Well, we'd better get to work then, hadn't we?" And she whipped a glittering pointy stick from nowhere and waved it around. In a minute the housework was done!

"Now for your carriage, horses and footmen," said the fairy.

She asked Cinderella to fetch a pumpkin from the garden, four mice and a fat rat from the trap, and two green lizards from under the doorstop. Cinderella stood there speechless as they were all transformed.

"Hurry, my dear," said her fairy godmother, "you'd better get going." She pushed Cinderella towards the open door of the carriage.

"But . . . what will I wear?" asked Cinderella, looking down at her raggedy work clothes.

"Oh! Silly me," said her fairy godmother, and she touched the top of Cinderella's head with her magic wand. When the tingling stopped, Cinderella peered into a gilt mirror that her godmother was holding. In the reflection she saw herself wearing an amazing shimmery gold dress. Round her throat sparkled a three-tiered choker, and a pearl tiara sat in her hair, which had been combed and piled on top of her head. The only thing wrong was her bare feet poking out from under the dress!

"Oh, don't worry about your feet, I have these." And her fairy godmother bent down and placed a glass slipper on each foot. They fitted perfectly. "Now remember, you must leave before midnight when the spell will be broken and everything will return to normal."

"I won't forget, I promise. Thank you so much." Cinderella hugged her fairy godmother and climbed into the carriage.

Soon Cinderella's carriage pulled up in front of the towering palace, and the footmen jumped down to open the door.

As she entered the breathtaking candlelit ballroom, everyone stopped and stared, including her stepmother and stepsisters. Nobody recognized her. Everybody assumed that she was someone of vast importance.

If only they knew. . . . Before she could even worry about what to
do next, someone tapped her on the shoulder.

"May I have this dance, please?" It was the prince himself, bowing to *her*.

"Y-yes, your highness." She was blushing like mad, but she managed to
curtsey. From that moment on, it was as if they were the only two people in
the room and they danced every dance together.

Before she knew what was happening, Cinderella suddenly heard the clock start chiming twelve – oh no! She'd forgotten!

"I must go," she whispered to the prince and, reluctantly letting go of his hands, she hurried out of the ballroom.

"But I don't even know your name!" called the prince.

Cinderella ran as fast as her heavy dress would allow, almost falling down the front steps of the palace in her effort to reach the coach.

In her hurry to leave, one of her glass slippers came off, but there was no time to stop, she had to leave it behind. Just as she touched the door of her carriage, it disappeared and all that was left in front of her was the pumpkin, the lizards, the rat and the mice. Cinderella found herself dressed in her ordinary clothes once again. Only the one glass slipper remained. She put it in her pocket and as she walked home, she thought, *That was the best night of my life.*

The next day Cinderella was in a daze as she made breakfast and brought it into the dining room. The same old bickering and orders followed . . . but Cinderella was too happy to care about all the commotion this morning. She had a secret – she had danced with a prince!

The rest of the day passed in a blur for Cinderella but at dinnertime she was shaken out of her dreams by the sound of the doorbell. Who could that be? It was a royal messenger with a servant standing behind him.

"Can you gather together everyone from this house? I have an important announcement," he said rather pompously, as Cinderella led him down the hall. When Cinderella, her stepmother and her two stepsisters were all standing before him, the messenger unravelled a scroll and began to read.

"By order of the Royal Prince, every lady in the land shall try on a glass slipper that was left behind at the palace last night. The prince shall marry whoever the glass slipper fits."

Well, bedlam broke out in the hall – the two sisters ran screeching like geese into the sitting room and fought for space on the velvet sofa while Cinderella hovered nervously behind. *Would they let her try?*

Camilla presented her bunion-covered foot and tried to force the slipper on it. Of course it wouldn't fit!

Clarissa laughed. "Mine's sure to fit like a glove!" But her foot wouldn't fit either – it must have been her large hairy toes. Both girls were rudely demanding another go when the messenger spotted Cinderella.

"Now you, young lady," he said, ignoring the sisters' protests as the servant brought the slipper over to Cinderella.

"What? Her? How can she? She's a servant!" shouted her stepmother as she jumped up to stop Cinderella from trying the slipper on. But it was too late. Cinderella sat down on the sofa and slid her foot easily into the glass slipper. It was as if it had been made for her, which of course it had.

"I've got the other one here," she said smiling shyly, and she took the matching slipper from her pocket.

Her stepmother and ugly sisters watched, mouths open, as Cinderella was escorted to the palace to meet her prince. He took one look at her and, taking no notice of her threadbare clothes, got down on one knee to propose. She looked into his eyes, saw the kindness there and knew instantly that he would make a wonderful husband, so she said yes!

The following weekend there was the biggest wedding the kingdom had ever seen. Cinderella wore a gorgeous dress made by her fairy godmother. The bodice was embroidered with crushed diamonds and there were tiny pearls around the neck that matched the jewels in her tiara. Her skirt and veil were made from ivory gossamer, spun by exotic spiders that had fed on milk and liquid gold.

It was the dress of a true princess bride, and as she walked down the aisle with her prince, Cinderella knew that she would never have to scrub a coal cellar again in her life!

Cinderella's Accessories

Grab a grown-up

Every princess MUST have sparkly accessories – it's the law!

Cinderella's Sparkly Three-Tiered Choker

You will need

A roll of thin elastic thread • Glittery beads •

Lots of sequins in different colours •

50 cm of silver-sequinned trim •

Needle and thread • Press-studs

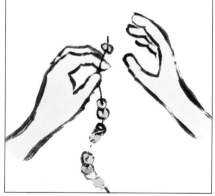

1. Measure the elastic round your throat so it fits closely but not too tight. Add an extra 10cm for tying later on. Cut another piece of elastic to the same length.

2. Thread one piece of elastic with different coloured sequins. Measure it round your neck to make sure it fits snugly, then tie the ends in a double knot.

3. Now thread the second piece of elastic with both sequins and beads in an interesting pattern. Make sure it fits round your neck before tying the ends in the same way.

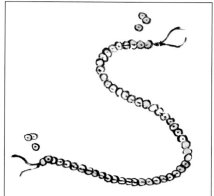
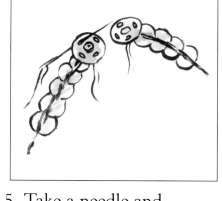

4. To make the middle tier, measure the sequinned trim round your neck – add 2 cm extra. Take off three sequins at each end and tie knots to stop the rest falling off.

5. Take a needle and thread and sew on the press-stud – one half on each end of the sequinned trim. Ask a grown-up to do this as it is rather fiddly.

6. Put the sequinned and beaded elastic round your neck first, and then the silver trim. Last of all add the sparkly sequinned choker. How glamorous is that?

Now you've learnt how to make the choker, why not make some bracelets or armlets to complete the glittering princess look? Using the same principles as above, you can either make the bracelets match your choker or go for a total contrast in colour and design. Don't just stick at three – how about 20!

Just make sure you are wearing your best clothes to get the maximum Cinderella transformation effect!

The Magic Mirror

Grab a grown-up

After you have made up your beautiful princess face and have teased your hair into all sorts of gorgeous styles, you probably want to look at how lovely you are. So, why not make yourself a magic mirror that fits stylishly in your room. Get all your friends to bring a mirror tile with them to your party.

You will need

Mirror tile • Thick card • Scissors • Strong fabric glue • Glitter • Other small shiny objects like stones, sequins and buttons • Lots of coloured beads • Pretty ribbon

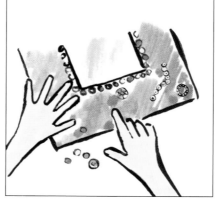

1. Place the mirror tile on the card. Measure and draw a border around the tile on the cardboard. Carefully cut it out with your scissors. Glue the mirror down on to the centre of the cardboard.

2. Decorate the frame with different coloured beads, little fancy buttons, and sequins in any pattern you like. Put glue in any remaining gaps and cover the whole frame with glitter. Leave to dry flat.

3. If you want to hang the mirror, ask a grown-up to help you make two small holes at the top of the frame. Thread some pretty ribbon through the two holes and tie the ends together in a knot.

Mirror, Mirror on the Wall!

Now, hang it up and look in the mirror. No need to ask, "Who is the most beautiful princess of all. . . ?"

YOU
ARE!

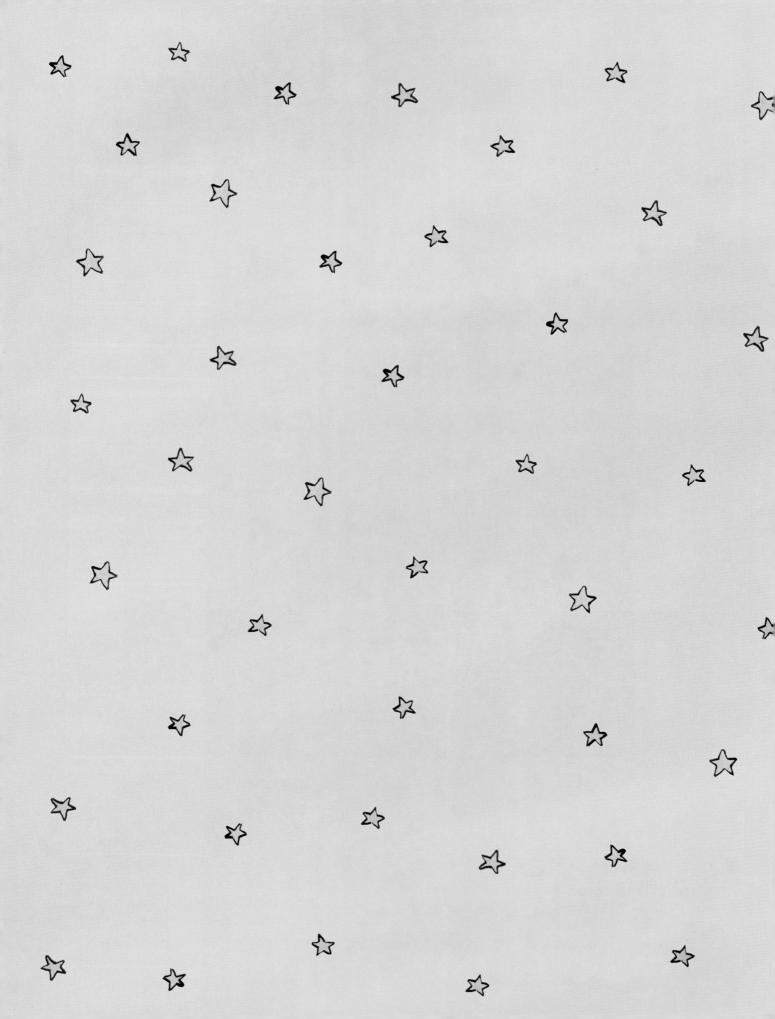